A NOTE TO PARENTS

When your children are ready to "step into reading," giving them the right books is as crucial as giving them the right food to eat. **Step into Reading Books** present exciting stories and information reinforced with lively, colorful illustrations that make learning to read fun, satisfying, and worthwhile. They are priced so that acquiring an entire library of them is affordable. And they are beginning readers with a difference—they're written on five levels.

Early Step into Reading Books are designed for brand-new readers, with large type and only one or two lines of very simple text per page. **Step 1 Books** feature the same easy-to-read type as the Early Step into Reading Books, but with more words per page. **Step 2 Books** are both longer and slightly more difficult, while **Step 3 Books** introduce readers to paragraphs and fully developed plot lines. **Step 4 Books** offer exciting nonfiction for the increasingly independent reader.

The grade levels assigned to the five steps—preschool through kindergarten for the Early Books, preschool through grade 1 for Step 1, grades 1 through 3 for Step 2, grades 2 through 3 for Step 3, and grades 2 through 4 for Step 4—are intended only as guides. Some children move through all five steps very rapidly; others climb the steps over a period of several years. Either way, these books will help your child "step into reading" in style!

www.universalstudios.com

www.randomhouse.com/kids

Library of Congress Cataloging-in-Publication Data
Corey, Shana.
Brave pig / by Shana Corey ; illustrated by Christopher Moroney.
p.   cm. — (Step into reading. A step 1 book)
SUMMARY: When the Boss disappears into the scary cellar, Babe the pig thinks that he is in danger and goes to the rescue.   ISBN 0-375-80204-5 (pbk.) — ISBN 0-375-90204-X (lib. bdg.)
[1. Pigs—Fiction. 2. Farm life—Fiction.]
I. Moroney, Christopher, ill. II. Title.
III. Series: Step into reading. Step 1 book.
PZ7.C8155Baaj 1999 [E]—dc21 98-53768

Printed in the United States of America   November 1999   10 9 8 7 6 5 4 3 2 1

Step into Reading®

Brave Pig

by Shana Corey

illustrated by Christopher Moroney

Based on the character Babe created by Dick King-Smith

A Step 1 Book

Random House 🏠 New York

Babe loves the grass.

He loves the sky.

He loves the sun.

Babe loves cows
and sheep
and dogs.

He even loves the cat.

But there is
one thing that
Babe does NOT love...

The cellar!

The cellar is cold.

The cellar is dark.

The cellar is scary!

"Hello,"
Babe says.
Hellooooooo,
says the cellar.

Babe runs away!

Oh, no!
The cellar is
eating the Boss!

Babe is scared.

But Babe is brave.

Babe goes
down,
down,
down,
into the cellar.
BANG!
The doors shut
behind him.

It is dark.

It is cold.

Where is the Boss?

CRASH!

The cellar is trying

to get Babe!

Help!

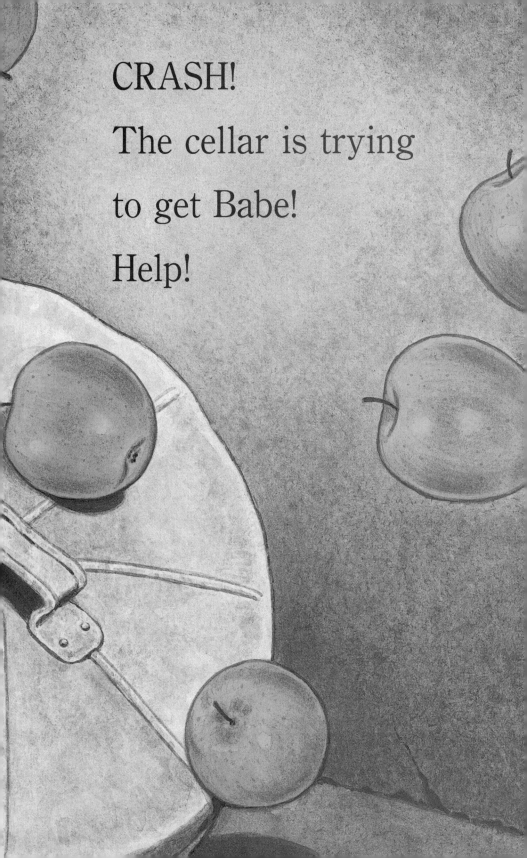

The light goes on.

Babe sees the Boss.

"Oops,"

says the Boss.

Oooooops!

says the cellar.

"Listen to that echo,"
says the Boss.
Echooooooo!
says the cellar.

The Boss laughs.

Babe laughs.

The echo laughs.

Babe helps the
Boss out of the cellar.
What a brave pig!

Now Babe loves
everything—
even the cellar!